# ICE CREAM WITH GRANDPA

A Loving Story for Kids About Alzheimer's & Dementia

BY LAURA SMETANA

ILLUSTRATED BY ELiSABETE B. P. De MORAeS

Guide for Parents and Caregivers: Tips for Talking with Children About Dementia, Hospice, Death, and Grief by Diane Snyder Cowan, MA, MT-BC, CHPCA

FLYING CARDINAL PRESS

Ice Cream with Grandpa
A Loving Story for Kids About Alzheimer's & Dementia

Published in 2022 by Flying Cardinal Press, LLC, Woodridge, Illinois.

Library of Congress Control Number: 2022901128
ISBN: 978-1-7371409-2-4 (hardcover)
ISBN: 978-1-7371409-4-8 (paperback)
ISBN: 978-1-7371409-5-5 (ebook)

Edited by Jennifer Rees
Book design by Kath Grimshaw

Guide for Parents and Caregivers: Tips for Talking with Children About Dementia, Hospice, Death, and Grief © 2022 by Diane Snyder Cowan, MA, MT-BC, CHPCA

The artwork in this book was rendered with digital watercolor.

To my dad (Grandpa Brian) and my son,
Stirling, with all my heart.
And to those with Alzheimer's and other dementias,
and all who lovingly care for them. —L.S.

To my parents, Zulmira and Antonio, for always
having taught me important values in life. They're
my foundation. To my wonderful husband, Jairo, and
beloved daughter, Anna, who always encouraged me
to follow my dreams. —E.B.P. de M.

When I was a baby, Grandpa gave
me my first taste of ice cream.
I loved it from my first lick!
After that, every time we visited
Grandpa's house, I got ice cream, too.

Grandpa taught me about all kinds of flavors that made my tastebuds smile.

There was vanilla,

strawberry,

mint chocolate chip,

and—Grandpa's favorite—rocky road.

We had ice cream in bowls, cones, and sometimes, we ate it in the kitchen cabinet.

Grandpa also taught me about gardening.
Together, we planted flowers, vegetables, and fruit trees.
He showed me how to care for them, too.

When our crops were ready to harvest,
Grandpa helped me transform them into
tangy salsas and sweet, sticky jams.

On warm summer days, Grandpa took me to the park.

He pushed me on the swing,

caught me at the bottom of the slide,

and played tag with me.

When I got a little older, Grandpa needed a cane to help him walk. He couldn't run around as much, but he liked to watch me play. When the ice cream truck came, his eyes lit up. "Go get one for you and one for me," he said with a wink. We sat side by side and licked away in the blazing sun before it melted.

When it was too cold to play outside,
Grandpa read me books.

We tried on all his silly hats and
played hat shop together.

He told me stories about his childhood on a farm over big bowls of ice cream.

When I was your age, I had to help my mom milk the cows before school.

He showed me postcards from his travel adventures, too. I wanted to see all the places he visited.

Gradually, Grandpa started to slow down.
His knees hurt so much that he couldn't garden,
take me to the park, or travel anymore.
He had surgery to fix his knee, then his back
and wrist. After each surgery,
we visited him in the hospital
and helped him recover
at home.

Soon, Grandpa couldn't live by himself.
He decided to move to a new place with people
his age and caregivers who could help him out
every day. I was sad he had to move, but Mom
said, "It will take some getting used to, but I bet
we'll find new things to enjoy there."

HOUSE
FOR
SALE

On my first visit, I didn't know where to go or what to do. The building looked like a fortress. We signed in at the front desk and walked down a long hallway with doors. Grandpa was waiting for us. His apartment was small. It had the same furniture, pictures, and hats. But I still missed his old house.

"Do you want to check out the ice cream parlor with me?" Grandpa asked. "Yes!" I almost shouted. I couldn't believe my eyes. There was a real ice cream shop just down the hallway!

We ordered two scoops of vanilla for him and the flavor of the month for me. It became our special place.

After a few months, Grandpa's knees started bothering him again, so I went to the ice cream parlor by myself. On my walk back to Grandpa's apartment, the other residents waved and said, "That's a lot of ice cream for one kid!"

"One is for me, and one is for my grandpa," I replied proudly.

"He's lucky to have you!" they said.

*I'm lucky, too,* I thought.

Soon, Grandpa stopped driving, so we started bringing him groceries and ice cream. There were other changes, too. Grandpa looked thinner, he didn't want us to stay as long, and he got tired more easily. He began to forget things and seemed confused.

One afternoon, I noticed he left the stove on and had fallen asleep. He was also forgetting to eat his meals and losing his balance. I was worried about him, and Mom was, too.

One day, Mom told me Grandpa would need to move to a new place called memory care. The doctor said Grandpa had dementia, a condition that was hurting his memory and making it hard for him to do everyday things. He would need more help.

"Will there be an ice cream parlor at Grandpa's new place?" I asked.
"I don't think so," Mom said, "but we can still bring ice cream for you both to enjoy together."

We packed up his things.
I was sad and angry that he had to move. I had just gotten used to everything, and now it was changing again.

His new apartment in memory care was smaller and there were new people. It took time for us both to adjust.

But soon, we both made new friends.
The people who worked there knew my
name, there were other kids who visited,
and Grandpa's new neighbors were friendly.
They even had parties with three-layer
chocolate cakes, warm cookies, and ice cream!

Grandpa started to change even more. He didn't want to leave his room for the parties, and sometimes he didn't believe we were his family. "That's not you!" he declared some days when we came to visit.

It made me sad and upset. Mom explained that dementia was changing how his brain worked and that was why he was acting different—it wasn't my fault.

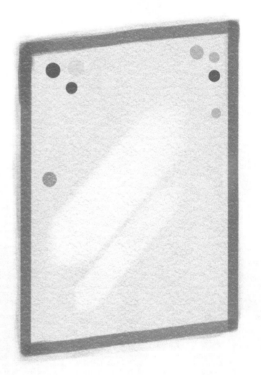

Sometimes I didn't want to visit Grandpa because I was afraid he wouldn't remember me.

"I know it's hard and that's okay. Sometimes, I feel sad and upset, too," Mom said. "Grandpa's mood and what he remembers may be different each day, but always know, Grandpa is still Grandpa. He still loves you. He can still feel our love, and we can still enjoy being together."

One day, Grandpa fell and broke his hip. He was too frail for surgery and wasn't able to get out of bed anymore.

On days he felt good, we played catch and told each other jokes.

What happens if the tram conductor drives upside down? The coins come out of his pocket!

Other days, when Grandpa was too tired to play or talk,
I drew him colorful pictures to hang on his wall.

After a few weeks, Grandpa was able to sit in a wheelchair. I gave him rides around the hallways. But he wouldn't be able to walk again, and he wasn't going to get better.

Mom said he was going into hospice care, which meant the doctors were going to focus on making him comfortable.

The next time we visited, Grandpa asked me for ice cream. But there was no ice cream parlor and no special event that day. I spotted a nurse in the hallway. "Do you have any ice cream?" I asked.
"It's for my grandpa."

She smiled and said, "Yes, we do have some today."
I followed her to the kitchen and watched as she pulled
open the freezer door. "This one is for your grandpa,
and this one's for you," she said with a wink.

Grandpa smiled when I returned. Together we enjoyed our cups of creamy chocolate ice cream. It tasted just as good as the first spoonful he gave me when I was a baby.

When it was time to go home,
Grandpa reached for my hand as
I said, "Bye, Grandpa, I love you."
His hand was thin, but his grip
was still strong.

"Bye," he said in a whisper as he squeezed my hand. And in that moment, I could feel the strength of his love surrounding me like rays of sunshine.

That was our last ice cream together. Grandpa died later that night. The next day, Mom and I shared our favorite stories of Grandpa. We laughed and cried. It felt like Grandpa was with us again.

That spring, we planted a tree in his memory. I still miss Grandpa, but now whenever I have ice cream, each scoop brings back sweet memories of our time together.

# A Guide for Parents and Caregivers:
## Tips for Talking with Children About Dementia, Hospice, Death, and Grief
by Diane Snyder Cowan, MA, MT-BC, CHPCA

**We'll get through this together.**

**I'm ready to listen if you feel like talking.**

**Let's talk about what would make you feel more comfortable.**

**I can just sit with you; we don't need to talk right now.**

Alzheimer's disease and other dementias can be overwhelming to family life. The impact of serious illness and death can be confusing for children, especially as they cope with school, peers, and changes at home. Often children are not equipped with the skills needed to manage big feelings. If unexpressed, feelings intensify and become more complicated for a child to master. Having conversations about dementia, serious illness, grief, death, and loss with your child may seem daunting but are critical to their well-being.

## General Guidelines

- **Use honesty and simplicity** when talking about the person with dementia or other serious illness. Use developmentally appropriate language. Tell children factual information to help them understand dementia and, later, that the person has died.
- **Allow time for repeated questions,** speculations, and the telling of the story. Children may need to hear the same information many times.
- **Be available to listen and initiate conversations.** Children need you to normalize their big feelings so that they feel safe expressing them. When listening, give your undivided attention.
- **Describe the feelings they can expect to have.** These might include feeling sad, angry, guilty, scared, or worried. Give examples of how you manage these emotions. Be honest about your own feelings.
- **Demonstrate and discuss appropriate ways to express feelings.** It is okay to share your sadness and tears with your children. Children may avoid activities or conversations to prevent family members from crying or feeling sad. Reassure them that it's okay if you cry after they say or do something, and that they are not responsible for your tears. Be sure they know that crying can help them feel better.
- **Understand that anger is important for children to express** and try not to take their anger personally. Give them ideas of how to let out anger without getting in trouble; for example, punch a pillow, go for a run, talk about it, etc. Feelings can also be expressed by writing, drawing, and making music.
- **Involve children in remembrance activities.** Collect photos, retell their stories, or create a memory box with mementos. In addition, make plans to remember your loved one on special occasions and holidays.

# Dementia Specific

- **Be honest and use clear, simple language.** Start the conversation as soon as your loved one is diagnosed. *Grandpa has an illness that affects how his brain works. It is hurting his memory and ability to do things.* Pictures of the brain, videos, and literature are helpful. Allow the child to lead the conversation and ask questions.
- **Address the child's fears.** Tell your child that dementia is not contagious. *You cannot "catch" it.*
- **Let the child know the person with dementia is still the same person** despite losses that are occurring. *As Grandma's brain changes, her reality and memory may change from day to day. She may forget things, but she still loves you and will still feel your love.*
- **Have a list of things to do with the person with dementia.** This will help create lasting memories and help children maintain a relationship with their loved one. Consider low-energy activities such as eating ice cream, coloring, doing simple puzzles, telling stories, or reading.
- **Explain changes in a loved one's behaviors. Remind the child that these changes are not their fault but part of the illness.** Explain delusions, changes in mood or personality, difficulty doing daily tasks, and asking repeated questions. Do not force interactions during times of distressing behaviors. Gently remove the child from the situation until things calm down.
- **Encourage, validate, and normalize feeling expressions.** The child may feel grief, anger, sadness, and experience a myriad of reactions.
- **Supervise visits** with the child and the person with dementia. Model appropriate behavior and language. Avoid phrases and words that can be distressing and isolating, such as: *Don't you remember...? Remember when...?*
- **Maintain connection** through illness and afterwards with legacy-making and remembrance activities.

**These conversations will be ongoing as changes will occur over the course of the disease.**

# Anticipatory Grief

Many of us are aware that grief is a normal part of the death experience, but grief also occurs prior to death, especially with losses that occur over time. There can be great benefits for both the person with dementia and with the family when anticipatory grief needs are identified and addressed.

- **Adapting to a new and ever-changing environment.** One aspect of dementia and other serious illnesses are that things are constantly changing, and losses are constantly happening. Identifying and acknowledging the loss and associated feelings helps. Talk about the new adjustments occurring with family and the person with dementia. This could include loss of daily living skills, communication, memory, placement or enrolling in hospice care.
- **Legacy and reflection techniques are one way of managing anticipatory grief.** Remembering and telling old stories, looking at old pictures, and listening to music, can elicit conversation with the person with memory loss. Decorating hand tracings results in a meaningful keepsake memento.
- **Explaining hospice to a child.** As hard as this is, start the conversation and get straight to the point. *It's time for Grandpa to have hospice care. Hospice care will help Grandpa feel much more comfortable and increase his quality of life.* Check for misunderstandings and invite the child to ask questions. Allow them to lead the conversation. Use books and videos about the life cycle and end-of-life. Ask your hospice care team for support.

# Death, Grief, and Loss

Grief is a normal, necessary, natural reaction to death and loss. It is unique to each individual. There is no right or wrong way to grieve. There is no calendar, no timeline, and no stages, but there is a roller coaster of physical, emotional, cognitive, behavioral, and spiritual reactions that everyone experiences in their own way.

- **Use honesty and simplicity.** Tell children factual information to help them understand that the person has died. Children are concrete thinkers and are often confused by metaphors such as *"Your Grandpa is sleeping,"* euphemisms, and complicated stories. Use the word "died." Let your child lead the conversation. You can begin by asking them what they know.
- **Be aware of magical thinking.** Children believe their thoughts can cause things to happen—they may believe that things they wished, said, or did, caused the person to die. They may also believe that the person is coming back. It is important to help children understand the finality of death so that they can grieve the loss.

- **Encourage involvement in memorializing activities.** Give choices about participation in the illness, death, and funeral. If possible, include children in planning the funeral or memorial services. Be sure to explain what will happen during various parts of the service.
- **Maintain daily routines,** as they provide safety and security.
- **As your child grows and develops, they may re-grieve** and ask questions as they process the death and loss over time. Children grieve according to their developmental level and understand the permanence of death as they develop abstract cognitive skills.
- **Encourage involvement in remembrance activities that honor and celebrate** your loved one. Remembrance activities provide children safe and constructive ways to express their grief. You can light a candle, visit the cemetery or other special place, eat their favorite foods on their birthday, donate to their favorite charity, create a memory garden, and take time to remember.
- **Do not lose hope.** Help your child carve out a special place in their heart for their loved one while helping them integrate this death into their lives. As they grow and mature, they may feel sadness with each milestone: graduations, family events, holidays, and other special times. Your openness and understanding through these times will be comforting.

## Additional Resources:

Alzheimer's Association
https://www.alz.org

National Alliance for Children's Grief
https://childrengrieve.org

Diane Snyder Cowan, MA, MT-BC, CHPCA is a leading national expert on grief and loss, and promotes grief support for children and adults at the national, regional, and local levels. In 2020, Diane retired from her position as the director of Western Reserve Grief Services of Hospice of the Western Reserve in Cleveland, Ohio, where she worked for twenty years overseeing on-site and community bereavement programs. In addition to working with and developing programs for patients with dementia throughout her career, Diane's father experienced early stages of vascular dementia prior to his death.

## Author's Note

This book was inspired by the relationship between my son and his grandpa, my dad, who died of Alzheimer's and vascular dementia. I am grateful to have been part of my dad's care team of family, friends, and medical professionals, and to have witnessed the loving bond between him and my son. While there were challenging days, there were also many moments of sweetness and joy as we learned to enjoy new ways of being together.

As experts say, once you've met one person with Alzheimer's and other dementias, you've met just one person—every person's experience is unique. According to the Alzheimer's Association, currently there are 50 million people living with Alzheimer's and other dementias around the world. While this book tells one story, I hope it helps other families and children navigate the challenges and joys that come with maintaining meaningful relationships with loved ones impacted by dementia.

## About the Author

**Laura Smetana** has fond memories of enjoying ice cream with her son and his grandpa, Laura's dad. This book was inspired by their relationship, before and after her dad developed Alzheimer's and vascular dementia. She has three generations of ice cream scoopers in her home—one from her grandpa, one from her dad, and one she got with her family in France. Each one brings back sweet memories with loved ones. Laura co-authored her debut children's book, *Little Squiggle's Lake Adventure*, with her son, Stirling Hebda. She lives with her family in the Chicago suburbs, where she is happily at work on several new books for kids. You can visit her at **www.laurasmetana.com**.

## About the Illustrator

**Elisabete B. P. de Moraes** loves to laugh. When she was a child, she looked forward to weekends when her grandfather came to visit and brought lots of candies. When she isn't illustrating picture books, you can find her streaming her favorite shows or sitting around the kitchen table with her family and friends, talking, laughing, and enjoying ice cream. Her favorite flavors are strawberry and salted caramel. Elisabete lives in Brazil with her husband, daughter, and their neighbor's cat, Cookie, who is always sneaking into their home. Soon they will have their own pet—they're just waiting for their daughter to decide between a dog, cat, swimming cow, or llama.

# BONUS keepsake ACTiViTY SHEET

Download your free keepsake "All About My _____"
activity sheet and art prompt to enjoy with your loved one at

www.laurasmetana.com/keepsake-activity

CPSIA information can be obtained
at www.ICGtesting.com
Printed in the USA
LVHW070833211222
735678LV00014B/515